KALEIDOSCOPE

"Colors of Life that deepen as you see a prism of events"

Daphne Stockman

Copyright © 2014 by Daphne Stockman. 669654
Library of Congress Control Number: 2014920595

ISBN: Softcover   978-1-4990-7675-2
        EBook   978-1-4990-7674-5

Scripture quotations from NSRV Bible are from the Holy Bible, King James Version (Authorized Version). First published in 1611. Quoted from the KJV Classic Reference Bible, Copyright © 1983 by The Zondervan Corporation.

Attribution-ShareAlike 2.0 Generic (CC BY-SA 2.0)—Gisela Giardino, Capisc, Xavier Caballe

All rights reserved. No part of this book may be reproduced or transmitted in any form or by any means, electronic or mechanical, including photocopying, recording, or by any information storage and retrieval system, without permission in writing from the copyright owner.

Rev. date: 02/11/2015

To order additional copies of this book, contact:
Xlibris
1-888-795-4274
www.Xlibris.com
Orders@Xlibris.com

TABLE OF CONTENTS

THE RED HOT ADVANCEMENT IN TECHNOLOGY 1

    Robot Revolt Year 2013 3

    Sequel To Robot Revolt 5

    Communication — 21st Century Style 7

THE GENTLE BLUE TOUCH OF WOMEN 9

    Women — Agents Of Change 10

    Mother Let Me Live! 11

    How Fair Is The Fairer Sex 16

THE CROSSROADS OF VALUES/VIRTUES AND DIS-VALUES IN OUR WORLD 18

    Save Canada. Save The Generations 19

    The Color Of My Skin 22

    The Face Of Haiti 24

KALEIDOSCOPE MEDLEY 27

    Memories Are Made Of These 29

The Red Hot Advancement In Technology

ROBOT REVOLT YEAR 2013

The Scenario

The World stood on its tail, almost at the brink of disaster.

There was chaos, with the economic crisis in Europe affecting other Nations. Industries and Companies were shutting down, leaving people without work. There were people hungry and sick. Water was scarce. There were unnatural alliances a number of them to avoid high tax payments. HIV was rampant, abortion was a daily occurrence. Same sex alliances thought to be the way to go was causing untold problems, where same sex partners were disagreeing and even resorting to murder to be free from this evil. The human being was not fit for living, so thought two scientists.

Violence was the name of the Game, because the 'law' was the survival of the fittest. All over the world one could hear the 'sound of violence'…loud bomb blasts, women shrieking and so forth.

In this Scene we find 2 brothers-Techno and Techni. They were scientists who were very savvy with technology. Their one objective was to deal with the' sound of violence' which they figured was causing too much angst and noise. They wanted to devise a system or a way of 'killing the enemy' who to them was the 'Imperfect human', in a soundless manner. No explosions or bombs or cries.

They kept this a big secret between them but occasionally discussed the topic in a general way between them.

In their laboratory they were trying experiments on how to destroy the enemy, the dictator, the avenger, the elderly, the sick in a quiet painless way. Was this possible??

They figured that they needed four Robots to help them in their work, so that the Scheme be kept secret and the master plan developed.

Techno and Techni added 4 Robots…..the names were Aye, Rhy, Cry and   Bots. These Robots were all humanoid with a wide range of skills to employ.

They could walk up stairs, show their feelings, sense the world around them and even decide what to do.

Robot means work and robots are machines that can work on their own. Using sensors they collect information and are able to record sound and take pictures.

They are very useful and can move. Robots have emotions in that they can interact with people and can display many expressions like happiness, sadness and anger.

The arms of a robot can sense the amount of pressure to put into a grip or handshake Robots are used in spheres like space, underwater, medical, on the mission to the moon and many others. They carry out a sensing of the world around and then act through the use of sensors. Sometimes they display what is beyond human intelligence..

Vision, touch, hearing used in robotics by contact switches signals to a computer through its sensor gauges. There are built in cameras for video and microphone for commands.

Artificial intelligence research is the brain of the computer which uses nerve networks to reproduce in a machine some of the brain of a human being. We can stop here for a while and ask. Will robots become intelligent? Will these machines run the world? Will machines get rid of human beings?

To grapple with these questions continue to read the story.

With the help of this team of Robots, Techno and Techni continued to research and discover how to proceed with a killing device without violence and noise.

Their objective was not to preserve life, unite or bring peace. Their objective was to kill off the human race, slowly but surely. Why did they want to do this.?.

It was because they figured that the human race had completed its course and in this had destroyed the world and humans themselves. They were not fit to live.

History is aware of scientists who kind of get focused on some strange theory or method and want to pursue it like a cat chasing a mouse. History has also termed some of this kind as 'mad scientists'.

In the special type of work taking place in the laboratory, the Robots were exposed to different types of vibrations which caused emotions and reactions within them.

For Techni and Techno, it was great working with Robots. There were no disputes, no waste of time or gossiping. They were told what to do and they did it.

Time went on and the scientists did discover a way of controlling violence but not avoiding destruction. This was because the method they devised had to enter the inner self of the person, or in other words, it had to go deeper than the skin.

They tried it out on animals and rodents and it worked. Just an injection or a Cookie framed with the substance and in no time the person or animal quietly fell over and collapsed without a whimper. The Robots worked and worked and all the while these vibrations, emotions and the substance being used were slowly entering their own inner bodies. Sometimes one or two of the robots were displaying odd motions.Techno and Techni were thinking that this was the result of too much to do for the 4 robots and since they were making profits in their science and work, they decided to get in another 2 robots. This went on for a number of years.

Techno and Techni were becoming popular and were invited to visit another country to speak about their new invention. They departed, leaving the 6 robots by themselves.

I mentioned about artificial intelligence......what is it? It is making machines do the things which would require intelligence of a human brain. It would make machines size up a situation and choose a sensible action. If the action was wrong, the machine would learn from its mistakes.

The six robots carried out their routine jobs as given but something strange was happening inside them. They were coming together and communicating what was going on.They had feelings of anger and sadness. Anger because their 'masters' were working them hard and pushing them around with fierce commands.

They shared sadness because what their artificial intelligence was telling them about the situation of killing off people needed a sensible action. They conferred and communicated and had nothing to lose in taking charge of the situation in this company. What they deemed as 'sensible action' was the overthrow of their' masters, because once they were out of the way, the robots could bring about 'sensible action'.

Let me explain the possible dangers of artificial intelligence to humans. What was happening was that the robots were being controlled by super intelligent computers. These six robots were able to move round.Communication and emotions were joining them together. I would like to refer to the movie 'Terminator' where we see killer robots getting rid of humans who were imperfect.

The same was happening in the 6 robots. They considered their masters as imperfect and cruel and getting rid of them would pave the way for the artificial intelligence machines to improve the situation or would they?

The plan was devised by Robot Cry. It was a Monday morning, when Techno and Techni stepped into the office and barely had they entered when the 6 robots surrounded them and with their long arms gripped their necks. Computers were flashing and the two humans could not move or call for help.

A loud bang emitted from the robots as they coughed out all the negative emotions which had held them for so long. In this chaos the master computer's signals of danger went off causing an explosion so destructive that both humans and robots disintegrated.

The story I have written is really something that may or may not come to pass in the future. However how far can we go with technology. Man is made for work, man is made with the gift of intelligence to be used…why make machines intelligent. By working only with machines, humans lose out on relationships but in today's world, perhaps it seems better to work with machines than humans for all the problems they bring like strikes etc. Are humans looking for a 'convenient' life? Computers and machines work much faster than a human brain and too much use of these will make humans too soft at the top. In fact one science fiction writer had said that humans are heading for imbecility.

The message of this story is that too much use of technology is detrimental. We have seen this in today's world Many nations are suffering the consequences of the wrong use or the over use of technology in their lives. Technology is not bad if used for the right purposes.

I like to think of Albert Einstein, Marie Curie, Musicians like Beethoven and others who used their human intelligence to discover science logic and truth.

These are things no super computer can do. Computers work according to programming rarely is creativity visible. Today we need creative minds that do not stop at the past or present but look into the future, keeping in mind the consequences of their creativity on the whole human race.

Thank you Robots for your revolt which brings an important message to the younger generation of humanity. All our gifts and talents and discoveries are given to us to develop and spread for the common good not just for more and more money.

Maybe we can ask a four-year old or even a 10 year old: "Who created the universe" and he may answer "God or a Super Being". After a few years (if human life is still around) you may ask him "Who destroyed the world" and he will answer "Greedy, heartless men who made money their God."

SEQUEL TO ROBOT REVOLT

Helping to Build a New World of Love

Excess technology and destructive cyber can definitely destroy the world and all that is in it. However our 'inner world' where we are truly who we are can never be destroyed.

Robot Revolt gave a message: That even machines like robots can detect those inner motivations of those who create them. This is what happened in the story. The robots detected the inner mind of the human scientists who were on a quest to destroy the whole human race because they were not fit to live. This is the motivation of "You're not OK" you need to go. Frankly in today's world this attitude is on when we see assisted suicide for elders or people very sick, when we hear of abortions, when we are overwhelmed with the tactics of one State for one religion at the destruction of others.

We see a similarity in history and the reality of today, when efforts were made to rid a certain race of anyone who was not 'pure' ethnic. Today ridding the world of all that is not one religion, one culture and one people are believed to be the "Ok" ones.

It is shocking to see how many young people came to the West from other parts, partook of their education, their privileges, only to return to their own countries to act against the country who befriended them. This is not being human but being evil, it means entering an attitude of "You're not Ok..I'm not OK (Eric Berne). Operating in this attitude means doing things that express hatred, carelessness and what is devoid of conscience.

What is the solution then to reversing this attitude? Will air strikes, war on the ground, bombs, missiles, rockets change this attitude which is at the bottom of much evil?

We have lost the battle already...why? Because we may have got our targets and destroyed them, but generations hence will still grow up in the same blind attitude, taught by their ancestors and so this goes on and on.

Is there then a solution? Yes a large dose of LOVE has to be injected into everyone.

We all have to join hands to BUILD A NEW WORLD OF LOVE

It cannot be a West versus East, East versus West. It cannot be North versus South and South versus North. It has to be a N/S/E/W combine and then only will it work. One person is needed to get this combination together perhaps at risk.

Love is too limited in our vocabulary.....Love in its true sense has two points:

1) Love shows itself in deeds rather than words
2) Love is a sharing of everything. It is not only 'taking' but giving.

I very often think to myself Why is the Islamic World so bent on destroying the West? Of course we have to discern what is Islam and what is fanatic Islam. Is it revenge for "Desert Storm", is it the permissive culture that militates against their own, is it because of religion (well all these years there seemed to be no set religion that was followed in the West according to some people). To tackle this and bring about sharing, we need forgiveness. The question is who will be first? Maybe this is not necessary at this stage.

As far as I can see there needs to be dialogue. The forces who want a separate State are only determined to get Power and with that the right to dictate and oppress which perhaps they feel will give them a place in the world. When we look back we see how many from one side have been killed and so retaliation is being used. Also after the death of their leader the Al Kaida were weakened and to my mind they have rounded up the class normally of hunters and animal killers to intimidate the enemies.

If these fanatics want their own State why not let them have it after negotiation with their neighbours or is there fear that they will try to take over. This battle which is leading to war must be halted because the forces involved will destroy the world.

What inner feelings do our robots transmit to us as we talk on this matter.

Sharing: What can the sides share besides arms. Love is not the mushy word that society has made. Love is really putting oneself in the other's shoes, developing communication not combat. Sharing what is good and acceptable in different cultures and avoiding the artificial types of culture which spring devoid of moral sense.

Young people in schools and colleges need to take this to heart. In colleges what type of mindset, behavior and culture do you show to immigrant students? Immigrants always have the tendency to feel left out. On the other hand if immigrants come to study and benefit from the West, they ought to merge with the society as a whole, keeping their own but not expecting to turn their immigrant world into their homeland.

Let us mull over the story of the Robots and reflect on the sequel for further inspiration to avoid a full scale War.

COMMUNICATION—21ST CENTURY STYLE

Today's most popular tool of communication is texting. You need a mobile phone, i pad, touch screen, apps, pager which are conversation gadgets to carry in one's purse or pocket. Many people allow their gadget to beep, play a line from a song or just ring. This always seems to happen at awkward times…in church, while one is driving or in a conference unless you put it off. Whatever…some put off the ringer and depend on feeling the vibration of the instrument that is trying to announce the call.

In most public places, like malls, public transport, even walking on the street one can espy many people looking at something in their hands and texting. This can go on for hours.

The language today for communicating is most of all short misspelt words, composed on how the word sounds e.g. How R U? Supposed to be 'How are you'

We have lost our charm for well-phrased sentences to convey a thought or a picture of an event or experience. We have lost the view of a face/s to read feelings and responses.

This type of tech.communication, as I call it, leads to isolation or at most limited encounters. If one talks to a teenager one just gets 'Yes', 'No', 'Maybe'.

When I ride the bus, I notice who is doing the talking. At least in my experience it is the older adults whom you can engage in conversation not the younger ones. Of course there are some exceptions, if you are lucky.

There are many advantages for this tool of communication. Faster messages, keeping occupied, dealing in emergencies. Parents keeping in touch with their kids. Reaching the whole world in fact, if you wish. I would like to mention that social media like Face book, Twitter and Email have made the world a smaller place. I can keep in touch with family back in my homeland through Face book.

Twitter affords a forum for exchange of views. Email is an online tool for sending and receiving messages.

Now there is no room for writing letters and sending cards. In fact cards can be sent online as well. A 'certain touch of class' and descriptive expression is missing and what a pity! Post Offices are either closing down or downsizing as the volume of mail has diminished except at Festival time.

So we are growing into a Culture where

> Texting versus Conversation
>
> Emails versus letter writing
>
> Language versus signs, symbols and abbreviations
>
> Conversation is reduced to Yes or No.

I met a young boy called Marco, a 7 year old. As he woke up he reached for his I phone and kept punching the keys. No conversation. After his breakfast he went on WiFi, then back to the I pad to watch video, then TV till lunch. Again in the evening the same routine.

Can you visualise this child at 10, at teenage? Unless attending a School changes him what is his future?

Here we can see it from two angles. This type of living will make him some sort of anti-social, because he will find he cannot talk so well. His ideas are very good but he is unable to express them.

The Technological Future needs to keep a balance especially for school children.

Nowadays they have a very short interest/concentration span. I am not saying ban iPhones, iPad etc. I am saying teach children how and when to use them.

Why? Because youngsters are mostly cared for by grandparents when parents are away at work and they (grandparents) do not understand how to use this technology and this leaves the kids on their own to make decisions as to what they need to text etc. Maybe these gadgets can be used, not all the time but when needed.

The future of technology is on….it will develop more. Each year we see how 'new' gadgets are on the market. We see how Tech. Companies vie with each other to bring out a new gadget. We see how the public just goes wild to obtain them. However very little thought is given to the type of individual this communication culture is encouraging. There are then those 'cyber terrorists' or cyber thieves who haunt the system and create hacking and cause constant change of passwords so one cannot remember a recent pw change.

Instead of communication being talking, listening and responding it has become a 'clicking' business employing both hands, eyes riveted to the instrument which could and has caused many accidents and mishaps.

Let technology not become an IDOL but rather a TOOL for good communication leading to conversation and encounter face to face (using Skype?)

The cost of using technology too has skyrocketed and this leaves two classes of people: Those who can afford and those who cannot. And we are back in the same imbalance in society which is never a good thing because it leads to deprivation and ends in protest.

The Gentle Blue Touch Of Women

WOMEN—AGENTS OF CHANGE

In the 21st Century of civilization, with such mind boggling inventions and achievements by people in most parts of the world, humankind feel good and uplifted and rightly so. Yet, when you look closer at countries in the world, what you see and hear brings sadness and a sense of frustration. Women, especially, are the victims of domination and exploitation, even till today. In third world countries starvation, disease and impoverished conditions are experienced by women.

In first world countries, women too, suffer starvation, disease and conditions that make them lose their value, though too often these are of another kind affecting them psychologically and emotionally.

It is not easy to address these issues of women in the world. To use force and negative expressions of protest would only have a counter effect in bringing about change. Woman's ability to lead and to rise up together as agents of change in the situations they face seems to be the answer as can be seen in the examples described below.

On March 11,2010, Mary Hanson(85), Kay Waldner(87), Olive Purdy(87). Bernie Glowe(85) and Violet Driscoll(88) were honored at Queen's Park in Canada. These women are the survivors of a small arms factory in Lake-shore where they, with others, were producing weapons during World War II for 50 cents an hour. Their hard work and dedication, it is told, helped the allied forces win the war.

In 1980 in a small village, close to the town of Ranchi in India, a group of tribal women raised a protest in a very creative way. They protested the drinking habit of their men folk. Drunkenness is one of the social evils in society which results in daily wife beatings, violence and poverty in the home. The tribal area is a wooded forest with plenty of tall trees. The women got together with police support and took up their stand each hugging a tree. This action had a sobering effect on the men folk and many gave up the habit of drinking slowly but surely. It was reported in Face book some time ago that a woman, named Tagger, aged 29 traveled to earthquake devastated Haiti to rescue her husband, Edure N St Louis who was left injured and homeless as his house collapsed. Tagger was able to convince the immigration authorities at the Canadian Embassy in Santos Domingo to grant Louis a visa.

In New Delhi, India, March 2010, a historic woman's reservation bill was passed by Rajya Sabha (Parliament). This bill reserves a third of all seats in Parliament and State Assemblies for women. For years women have fought for this recognition. They are to be honored for their perseverance in bringing about this change in Indian society through their peaceful protests.

In Mississauga, Ontario, Canada, a group of retired women spend time driving sick women to doctors and clinics. They not only come and get the patients but also wait for them till they are done. What a gesture of generosity to the community by bringing change in the life of elders and the disabled, who find it difficult to move around.

I have chosen examples of simple women to show that everyone can make a change. It would be unfair to omit the millions of mothers and wives who not only work 9 to 5 but come home and cook, take the kids to extracurricular activities after school, do the laundry and clean up. There was a movie on TV showing the women leaving town for a week. The men were in charge.

There were fathers with tiny babies, quite confused as to what to do, even though the women had left notes for them. Some men struggled in the kitchen. Well, you know what, the wives received a warm appreciative welcome when they returned. The movie did display a change in the attitude of the men. Although just a film, it captured the reality of women bringing change to a situation.

There are numerous women, who through their own ability have achieved great success. There are our women astronauts in Canada, others have their own business and some are writers and artists. In their achievements they have brought about change in the social milieu. A women who brought social change par excellence, was Agnes Gonxha Bojaxhui born in Skopje, Albania in 1910. At the age of 12 she wanted to help the poor and so travelled to Dublin where she joined the Loreto Order of nuns. Her professed name was Teresa. She was a teacher in Calcutta, now Kolkata, in India from 1929 till 1946. Priority was education, especially for girls at that time, as it still is. The school she taught in was a prestigious one but overlooked a slum, which seemed to beckon her. The call to serve the poor thus motivated her to found the Missionaries of Charity whose purpose is to serve God in the poor. Her role as an agent of social change, together with her companions, was to give dignity and hope to the poor in the gutters. People who lay dying on the streets were cared for in dormitories and given the chance to die with dignity. Many of them recovered with the help of the care received. Who would have picked up babies from the dust bins and loved and nurtured them to life? Many of these babies have been adopted by people in the western world, which is another example of change.

These examples are just a few to illustrate how women, in spite of so many odds, like discrimination, violence and exploitation have stood up with courage and perseverance Woman's creativity, dedication, skills and perseverance have won them praise throughout the centuries. Women can surely be acclaimed and honored because they have become the bravest agents of social change in different countries of the world.

One may ask why these women became agents of change:

1. The situation demanded action

2. The women were called or challenged and they stood up to it.

3. Women involved other women in their work, thus motivating the community. One may ask what were the values they practiced in these situations.

Love for the community stands out, then faith in the cause and courage

Women stand up and become Agents of Change in your city, region and nation. Let those who have brought change, inspire you to achieve the freedom you are seeking for and pursuing for so many years.

International Women's Day is celebrated on 8th March each year and you are invited to spread the message of Hope and Change to other women in the world.

MOTHER LET ME LIVE!

Part I: The Story

She got pregnant….that was Deena, a first year college student, an only child of parents who had divorced when she was a teenager. Deena was extremely attractive, with black hair and blue eyes and a feminine posture, but a person with a lot of anger, which came through when she spoke out on topics like pre-marital sex and other controversial subjects.

From teenage she lived with her mother, who had to work so hard to keep the house going. There was no quality time for her to sit and talk with her daughter, so the relationship between them drew a part. Deena was virtually on her own except for her meals and stay.

In college there was lots of 'fun' and activities but Deena felt envious of her companions who sported things like designer clothes, bags, and shoes . This tended to isolate her somewhat until she met Dicky, also a college student. They became very good friends and fell in love. Deena and Dicky became inseparable. Dicky too was the son of divorced parents . They both had much to share with each other about their experiences and feelings as young people.

It was the winter of 2008 after a night of 'fun' and sleep over with other college students, Deena felt something was not quite right. The hangover caused her tremendous discomfort. It was a month later she discovered that she was pregnant. Questions arose in her mind but the answers were vague and unanswerable. Deena revealed her condition to Dicky who was very perturbed.

Deena's childhood had been quite a happy one before her parents broke up. She missed her father but these were just memories now. What should she do in this predicament? The consequences of disclosing her pregnancy would bring untold anxiety and sadness to her Mom. Her friends would label her naïve. Deena and Dicky wanted to go for abortion. After all, they thought incorrectly, the child in her womb had not yet formed.

Deena was going through a terrible agony of conscience...should she, should she not? It was well over two months since she conceived. Dicky seemed to avoid her now. To ease her tension and fear she took a walk in the park and sat on a bench. It was then she heard a cry, a painful wailing, a childlike cry. She shook her head, turned around but the cry became louder until she realized that it was coming from inside her. Listening carefully this is what she heard:

MOTHER LET ME LIVE!!

I AM CRYING FROM YOUR WOMB!

Mother, you and Papa loved me into that small speck into which the Creator breathed life so lovingly.

I have grown to almost two months. Now darling Mom, I hear you are about to ABORT me... I cry out to you...... "Mother let me live"

I am beautiful like you and will be strong like Papa, please, please let me live!

Can you picture me, a sweet smiling babe, and then me a tot? What joy I would bring to you both and the family. In school, I would try hard to make you proud of me. In my teenage, I would never leave you.

I would be grateful for life – the life you both have been instrumental in giving to me.

Mother, please let me live....please do not KILL this little one who is eager to see you and the world around and who is eager to sing and play with other children. MOTHER LET ME LIVE!

Moreover, when I grow up, marry, and have my own child, won' you be happy to be a grandma!

MOTHER , DARLING MOTHER, PLEASE LET ME LIVE! I AM YOUR FLESH AND BLOOD – I LOVE YOU…..PLEASE LET ME LIVE! (A Cry from the Womb by the author…D.Stockman)

Deena knew the Cry came from her "baby girl". She broke down and was sobbing relentlessly. This was her 'baby', her child, begging to live.

As she kept sobbing, she felt a gentle hand on her shoulder. She looked up to see a kind grey haired woman standing by. The woman asked if she could help.

Deena told her the whole story and the cry she had heard from the womb. SHE JUST COULD NOT AND WOULD NOT KILL HER BABY. This was her Pro-Life decision, taken freely. She conveyed this to Dicky who, at first disagreed, but later accepted the decision. All babies who are aborted CRY in the womb to live, but many are not heard .

The Lady agreed to go and speak to her Mom and even offered her home for Deena to get over the pregnancy and birth. Of course there are many Pro life Centers available where kind people not only help the young mothers keep the child, but help them to learn how to bring up the baby. Ultimately, such mothers are helped to re-enter the social milieu again.

Deena and Dicky were married privately. They named the baby 'Rainbow' because she gave them Hope for a life of love together as a family. Rainbow grew up to become an accomplished Musician, focusing on the piano and became a celebrity in life.

Part II

Today there are many Deenas in our society and communities, but all do not heed the CRY FROM THE WOMB and make a Pro Life choice. What are the consequences of this? Before we go into that let us, look at history.

Throughout the ages, infants and children have been murdered endlessly within the womb and outside for no fault of theirs and their lives have been snuffed out like 'just lit' candles. It started with the order of Pharaoh "Every boy that is born to the Hebrews you shall throw into the Nile…..." This order was given because Pharaoh was afraid the Hebrews were more numerous and powerful than the Egyptians. (Exodus 1:8-22)

In the time of King Herod at the birth of Jesus, wise men from the East came to pay homage to the new King who was to be born according to their reading of the stars at Bethlehem in Judea. They met with King Herod who told them to find this king and inform him. However, the wise men returned to their country by another route. When Herod found he was tricked he ordered the massacre of children under 2 years of age. Why, because Herod wanted to be the only King in his territory and saw the birth of a New King as a threat to his power. It is heart rending to hear the cries of mothers at that time as expressed by the prophet Jeremiah

"A voice was heard in Ramah, wailing and loud lamentation. Rachel weeping for her children; she refused to be consoled because they are no more". These are examples of 'murder' of Babies newly born in the history of humanity who have paid the price for power and greed. In our age and time with education and technology, abortion of the child in the womb is rampant Moreover, this is 'Murder.' Yes, abortion is murder of a human being.

Facts To Ponder

Below is given some data to help the reader realize the magnitude of 'murders in the womb' taking place in our time. Globally each year over 40 million babies are aborted and on a daily basis the number is over 10,000. In United States. the yearly figure is over 2 million and daily more than 3500 babies are killed in the womb.

In Canada, more than 3 million have been aborted since 1969. In other countries, the number of abortions is in the thousands. NB.These are old statistics, today the numbers have increased.

Ontario Tax Payers pay $30 m. annually to end pregnancies.

China has a 'gendercide' policy. Chai Ling, founder of the Am.NGO All Girls Allowed believes this one child policy favoring boy over girl, besides being morally and spiritually debasing to China's culture and nation, has left 37 m girls missing with 32 m Chinese boys who will not have wives to marry!

HAVE WE GONE TOO FAR WITH DESTROYING THE GIFT OF LIFE???

Is this a 'Murderous' Generation? It is for you to conclude after you read this article. Keep the judgment to the One who gives life. Why is it that the human psyche desires destruction of life in all its aspects today?

Causes of abortion are almost 99% due to social reasons i.e. rejecting babies, not wanting them.

The relevant question people are faced with is when is the sperm impregnated with life. A lot of study and research has gone into this question and it has been scientifically proven that life starts from the moment of conception. Between conception and birth, references are made to 'mother', 'child', 'baby'. Where there is a mother there is a child and so as soon as fertilization takes place, conception takes place because it is at that moment the Creator implants Life into the sperm.

In today's world it has become so easy to take a person's life…we know the scenario:

Kidnap/Rape/Murder. Greed/Gain/Kill Hate/Ambush/Murder/Evil Powers/Control/Kill. In this scenario of Murder, does it seem OK to murder human life in the womb as well?

Hypocrisy and Contradictions

Our Society needs an overhaul. Much has been said about Change….but change can only come in an integrated manner. In our society when murder is committed the accused is given a trial and the deed is publicized and on the findings of the jury, the judge sentences the accused. When a woman deliberately murders her baby in the womb, it is a private matter. Why?…in both causes the crime is the same. In both cases, we are supposed to stand for justice and the right to live.

Isn't this an absurd system?

Young women who get pregnant out of wedlock, need to make a prolife choice and one reason they find it difficult is because society and the media go to lengths to again 'murder' the name of the woman. This is a contradiction and hypocrisy in that it is not only murder but also exploitation, If the mother has the right to abort or not, what about the child in her womb…..does he/she not have a right to live (Refer to the Cry from the Womb).

The contradictions in perspective are due to the lack of proper knowledge based on fundamental values of life: The 21st Century is experiencing a Conflict of Values in Life, which need to be addressed now so that future generations are not further confused and fall into the same pit.

Life is a gift from God. It is said that whenever a child is conceived and born, it means that God has not given up on human beings.

Article 3 of the UN Charter of Human Rights says

> **Everyone has the right to Life, Liberty and Security of Person'.**

Article 25.2 Motherhood and childhood are entitled to special care and assistance. All children whether born in or out of wedlock shall enjoy the same special protection

Life in the womb starts at the moment of conception and therefore abortion means destroying a human being.

Life in any form is gifted by the Creator. Suppose the Creator just recalls his gift of life? Where would you and I be? Our bodies would then be gone and our spirits would come before the Creator. What answer would one give to God when he asks "Where is your child"? He asked this question to Cain who murdered his brother Abel (Bible Genesis Ch.4:9/10…)

All countries are focused on the outer environment, in purifying the air, water, defending boundaries. What about the inner environment from which very often false thoughts and decisions emerge for the sake of vested interests? Are we so ignorant to think that the outer environment will improve without the inner environment changing to uphold the God-given values for which our ancestors toiled and labored?

In the area of health care, certain ethics prevail and these ethics are a systematic way of thinking on the values that are at work in the health care profession. Norms to protect these values are formulated. All values need to be experienced in order that they become valuable. Some value systems develop on someone else's conviction, but value systems ought to come out of one's own experience. Norms are concrete ways of making a value practical in life in the here and now.Norms are made on what is beneficial to the human being as God, the Eternal Source, has implanted in our hearts at birth through the natural law. Medical ethics affect life in three areas….the chief value being RESPECT.

Let us look at these values that are necessary for our whole life.

Life period	Value	Disvalue opposing the Value
Life at its beginning (conception)	Procreation	Contraception Artificial Insemination Abortion Genetic Engineering
Life during its course	Health/Healing to sustain and grow	Experimentation on human beings
Life towards its end	Respect for the dead Death concept moment	Transplantation Improper Life supports Euthanasia Pulling the plug too easily

All people of 'goodwill' need to check on moral ethical values. Make values your own by keeping on asking the 'whys', just do not remain passive. The source of all values is what is beneficial to the human being, as God the Eternal Source has imparted in the heart of human beings… it is God's law.

Our uniqueness, honesty, truth, values and norms to protect one another privileges us to be human beings.

Consequences Of Abortion On The Woman

The effect of Abortion on the woman is considerable. Many live with guilt and grief all their Life resulting in damage to themselves and others around them. Some experience constant bouts of depression and end up with psychological illness. Many need psychiatric treatment. To what purpose then is Abortion? It kills the child, a human person, and badly damages the Mother.

What Can Be Done To Protect Human Life In The Womb

Let me say here that there are many cases where miscarriages take place due to medical reasons, but a miscarriage is not abortion, because abortion is murder….on the basis of rejection of a human being due to social reasons

In this study we are talking about pregnancies as told in the story of Deena and Dicky.First and foremost there are a number of Groups who advocate prolife and help and assist theMother rehabilitate.

Women need counseling and support…can this be given?

Parents, Educators and young people need to meet in a forum and discuss the Truth about abortion and illicit sex.

Proper guidance on boy/girl interactions, dating etc need to be given. Media needs to look at their own values and ethics before undertaking to report on this issue.Parents at a very early age of the child need to work on giving their child what he/she Needs, not what he/she Wants ……because Wants make them indulgent and lacks discipline, which is needed in challenging life situations. Family Life needs desperately to be restored, where husband and wife do not divorce at the drop of a hat, but endure… for better/worse .. for rich/poorer and so forth.

A solid family base will prevent such type of 'murders in the womb'. Broken homes only aggravate the search for proper relationships leading to default in most cases.

Conclusion

Life is a precious gift for you and me and future generations. Let all people of goodwill safeguard it in all its forms by practising and promoting ethical values like those mentioned above . "Your children get only one childhood. Make it memorable."

This is a message for all readers of this presentation and for them to pass on……In the Bible, the book of Deuteronomy Ch.30:15 ff. God's invitation is given to choose which way to go. "Today I call heaven and earth to witness against you. I am offering you life or death, blessing or curse. Choose life so that you and your descendents may live in the love of Yahweh your God." (N.Jer.B).

HOW FAIR IS THE FAIRER SEX

In New York 1908 hundreds of women marched to protest working conditions of textile workers. They stood up for their working sisters in the Third World and refused to tolerate injustice and wanted change.

Each year on the occasion of International Women's Day (8th March), we look again at women in countries of the world but more than ever in parts of Asia. Take the Republic of India, there are different communities and tolerance is needed for everyone to appreciate the richness of their own as well as another's culture.

Tolerance is a very positive element in bringing society together in a possible growth towards integration in diversity. However when we come to society and women's role in it we need to question - Should we or should we not Tolerate?

Tolerance was chosen as a UN theme in 1995 -The Year of Tolerance but there was one area which got overlooked namely, what ought we NOT to tolerate in society.

When women are denied rights by being exploited and oppressed, when violence is rife and when self-determination is a far cry to freedom, then this beautiful positive tolerance does not exist, especially in countries which are fast developing economically and technologically. Where are the majority of women in society and are they being tolerated or are they meekly tolerating?

In this century even though many women have come forward to take responsiblity side by side with their male counterparts, domination and discrimination exist both in the workplace and family. A girl child has no rights.

A single woman, as far as some country's laws are concerned does not exist. Married women who are accepted in society become victims of violence and desertion when widowed, mostly because of inheritance. It is women from the middle class and poor people who become unequal members of the society. Gender inequality is too evident in all walks of everyday life. As a widow her right to her husband's property is divided and that too if she at all survives threats and violence by family members. The girl child suffers the 'son' syndrome. She has a deprived childhood. She is born as a burden for parents who have to amass a dowry to marry her off later. She is also the workhorse, the one who is fed less than the male and becomes an easy prey to sexual exploitation to survive. Prostitution continues because of rape, kidnapping, forced or duped allurement for jobs. Dowry and dowry deaths go on in subtle and unhidden ways even in high society.

A major fallout of the economic liberalization is the media's portrayal of women as commercial objects to be advertised. Last but not least many experiences show that women are the most cruel oppressors of other women with envy, back-biting and so on. The dehumanization of women is complete in this modern age of so called advancement. So the question is why in the face of all this do women continue to have TOLERANCE to bear up and refrain from protest.

What is at stake? Is it not women's dignity as a human person, created equal and given a role in life which is not secondary but complementary to the male. If women are not given their rightful place and dignity the human race will suffer because family life will be broken and fragmented. In fact we see this happening all around with a total disregard for human life and age old values which have worked well in the past. At stake as well is a growing civilization of life and love in which women alone can become their self-actualized selves to enable them to play the role of life bearers.

India and the World today need women as Agents who will be able to bring about change without violence and negativism. In the history of humankind, there have been many good examples of such women with faith, hope and love.

(Check the website to see details) There are many many women both in the East and West who are well equipped to reach out with their wonderful talents to their sisters in countries where they are suffering. As in 1908 when women stood up for their sisters in the Third World, so in the same way in this century there is need for women themselves to reach out to the millions of deprived women and empower them to live as human beings.

They would thus be agents of change in saving the human race from deterioration.

Agents of Change start with themselves, their attitudes and behavior, they start with the family, participate in women forums. I must say that there are many Agents of Change helping women in different parts but the need is for more such.

It is strongly advocated that women today cease to tolerate situations in society which dehumanize their gender and join to take collective action as needed. Much is being done as mentioned but a more concerted action is necessary.

The Crossroads Of Values/Virtues And Dis-Values In Our World

SAVE CANADA. SAVE THE GENERATIONS

Introduction

Canada is to be congratulated and honored for participating in introducing and promoting the 'Pacemaker'. Attempts to implant pacemakers to pace the heart beats with electrical impulses was made in 1892. Experiments and research to find a suitable pacemaker to pace the rhythm of the heart went on from 1899 to 1932 in America and was interrupted for sometime due to WW II. Canada's glory came when an external pacemaker was designed and built by a Canadian John Hopps in 1950,. He was an electrical engineer. Though the device needed simplification, nevertheless we find a Canadian in the long list of attempts made by doctors and others in Switzerland, US, France and Australia. The development of the pacemaker in dealing with cardiac problems and heart rate has saved millions of people and enabled them to live somewhat normal lives. Pacemaker implants are common in the Health System of Canada and are inserted with great skill. Statistics show that 3 million people worldwide have pacemakers and there are 600,000 implants done in a year. Canada is reflected in these statistics to a great degree. So we see how the Challenge of Research led to a way of helping heart patients 'live again'.

Today's Challenge

In our present times we encounter a great need which has appeared in epidemic form and that is AUTISM.

What is Autism?

It is a disorder of neural development where a child is not able to interact socially because of certain behaviour patterns. It occurs from a young age where the child is not able to process what the brain receives and where the brain affects the nerve cells. At one time this disease was not treatable but today there are numerous ways of trying to control Autism.

For further details please go http://discovermagazine or Wikipedia's website.

IS AUTISM CURABLE?

Diagnosis is needed fast because the early years of a child's life is crucial for cognitive, social and emotional development. (http://www.child-encyclopedia.com/en/importance -of-early-childhood-development/how-important-is-it. HTML

Yes, Autism is curable but it needs a lot money and patience. In Autism the whole body needs to be treated. It is not only a brain disorder but rather neural. The child suffering needs a diet with supplements which are all very expensive. Vaccines are needed.

Certain medication which is necessary bring about added reactions like pain and leaky bowel and others Treatment for Autism is unique because what works for one may not work for another. What is absolutely necessary is proper diagnosis and more information to help parents and caregivers.

This link will give information on treatment and common action..http://www.generationrescue.org/recovery.

A Family's Experience

This is the case of Ben......he was diagnosed on completion of age 4. It took his parents two years to enroll him in a Special Day Center.. Parents had to attend classes to learn about Special Need children. The wait to get Ben into Special Needs School was too long and brought about much anguish for the child and the parents. Support therapy and real and proper diagnosis was slow and there was no follow up of treatment.

Special Diet is needed for autism patients as the body cannot absorb certain foods. However this followed a 'hit and miss' kind of experience and was very, very costly. In addition Ben receives IBI (Intensive Behavior Intervention) therapy 5 days a week in a special program that is in partnership with the Peel School Board, called Section 23. Then again from a facility he has a therapist and 3 other therapists plus the services of a speech therapist.

At the end of their efforts to deal with Ben's case, his parents are in debt and on the verge of bankruptcy. Some parents do not have enough money to look into treatment and so the kids remain unattended and alienated.

Is There Hope That Cure Is Real?

Yes, very much so. There is a great breakthrough and it has been discovered that Stem Cell Therapy whereby there is a transplant of good cells into the Autistic patient is administered intravenously and subcutaneously. It is a painless procedure, it takes about 1 hour and gives no side effects. Dr. William Rader is the pioneer in this field.. However the cost of this treatment is too too high for middle class/poor parents. Further, stem cells taken from aborted fetuses is not ethical, but stem cell cultivated and grown in the laboratory may be the answer. Then there is the biomedical line which helps brings down the toxin load, helps the gut heal, boosts up nutrients and gets metal and toxins out of the system. This too helps cure. See the link again http://www.generationrescue.org/recovery.

What Is Being Advocated?

Parents, teachers and well wishers need to become aware and knowledgeable about Autism so that they may help the child as soon as autism is detected and not delay diagnosis and treatment.

Support and sponsor fund raising for this Cause. Suggested parent action:

Become an advocate for your child for you alone are the hope to get your child well recovered, by securing resources such as medical, health, nutrition and behavior experts.

What Can Canada Do?

We read about the great participation in the pacemaker development in Canada and how the Health System is supporting this intervention for its citizens. Now once again Canada, a nation of service and compassion, needs to treat Autism as a priority.

By including treatment for Autism in the Health Program of Canada.

Proper and swifter diagnosis/treatment/ongoing follow up (schools etc) Ongoing Research where this problem can be looked at in all its dimensions.......Medication, Therapy, Diet/Food, Supplements.

Also exploring ethical stem cell therapy, which in the long run would bring the cost down. Building Special Needs Schools for autistic kids Developing a method whereby kids are assessed before 3 years so that symptoms can be dealt with and speedier treatment administered.

All the above would need Special Clinics/Hospital to bring an integrated approach to Autism.

Urgent Message

Canada do it again. Become a Leader in fighting this problem of Autism which if not halted will lead to manpower being depleted in time to come. (See stats.)

In addition as Autism has become epidemic, it will leave girls/women unproductive, so what happens to future generations?

SAVE THE NATION CANADA
SAVE THE FUTURE GENERATION

THE COLOR OF MY SKIN

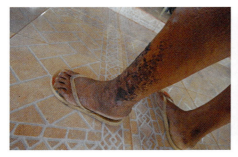  

I would like now to speak of THE COLOR OF MY SKIN.

In this world of 2014, with the World Powers claiming that their countries have people who are educated, well-established, technologically sound, economically improved and media experts, why are we still experiencing the Color Stigma? It is mostly the 'bold, fair and beautiful' in the society who get preference. What makes the Color of My Skin decide what I can do and what I cannot do because certain members of the society choose to call the norm for this decision. We are all aware of the old days when color prejudice was rampant but now in 2014 it is subtle and handled in a way which is not noticed unless you are the type that goes deeper into situations.

I have got to say that progress has been made especially when I see so many great newscasters and others chosen, not because they are different in the color of their skin. This is great. We need a greater emphasis to be made to fight this evil. A whole mindset needs to be changed……people of different color are P E R S O N S unique and gifted who need to be looked at the level of 'heart'. We still have a long way to go to get to this point and perhaps one day there will be a total change, because our young people are showing the way.

Let not the color of my skin be artificial, let not the color of my skin be lost, let not the color of my skin decide my future by pinning on me a false label.

The Heart of the Matter is You and Me regardless of color because we are meant to be one as humans on a Journey to our eternal home.

The Color Of My Skin!?

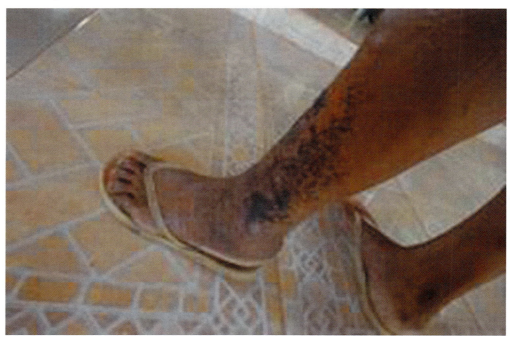

The sale of cosmetics has risen to high levels as we note the body lotions, facial creams, hair sprays, series of color dyes for the hair. All this to preserve the color of our skins and there is even a pack for removing wrinkles. Cosmetic sales touched $426 billion in 2011 and must have increased by now with new products of all kinds. Of course, and we must be truthful, many of us use the basics to enhance the 'skin' but there is always the temptation out there to try more and more of these cosmetics.

However there are some people in the society and on our planet who lose the color of their skin! How come you may ask.

Well think of this:

The Mining and Minerals Industry in Haiti extract US13 million of Bauxite, copper, calcium carbonate, gold and marble . A Canadian Corporation with its wholly owned subsidiary mined copper near Gonaives and exported 1.5 million tons of ore. The copper was valued at $83.5 million……..the Government of Haiti got about $3 million! In Lakwev, earth is dug from hand-made tunnels and washed for small bits of gold by local residents.

In this same mineralized area in the Dominican Republic Barrick Gold and Goldcorp open pit mining is going on, where adults and even children are employed.

This would all appear to be good from the point of the Industry, except that the ratio of benefit to the parties concerned reeks of Injustice. There is a huge gap between $83.5 million and $ 3 million. This is injustice in the distribution of goods and their worth.

However there is another type of Injustice perhaps not known to the world and that is the 'Color of the skin' of those who work in the mines. Because of the toxic effect of minerals, the skin of the workers (including children) peel away leaving sores and wounds which end up in 'loss of skin' altogether. Take a look of some of the pictures taken at the Barrick Gold and Goldcorp in the Dominion Republic!

'Losing the Color of my Skin' is not acceptable anywhere in the world. We ask some questions : What are mining industries doing to guard their workers from this type of 'skin injustice'? It is the duty of Industry to make sure that their workers are protected against the effects of pollution whether outside or inside a person and certainly if this

is stemming from their own industry, machines etc. Is there any compensation given to people who suffer miserably? An average worker earns $4.80 per day (39.175 gourds equal $1 US dollar. This is an old statistic, check the recent exchange).

With this poor wage people cannot get the necessary treatment and so they waste and die.

I on behalf of all good and right-minded people APPEAL to the UN

To look into this matter and publish the facts of what is happening to human beings who become tools for profit.

An appeal too to Governments who mine in that area to get the proper wage and amenities to overcome this health hazard which makes people of the poorest nation in the Americas 'Lose the Color of their Skin."

Let us listen to the words of M.Teresa

The Sin of Indifference:
So we don't know, or we don't want to know or we don't care to know.

THE FACE OF HAITI

The Fish Bowl

This is the story of a Fish bowl, in fact of three fish bowls, placed one upon another. The first is a fairly large one containing some Big Fish. The second bowl contains medium sized fish but the connection with the large bowl is just a narrow flow through. The third bowl is the smallest and contains many, many small fish,. in fact, the bowl is rather crowded. Here again the connection between the second bowl and the third is just a small narrow flow through..

The first bowl gets all the good things, like plenty of water, food and air, but the second bowl of fish have to scrounge for the particles of food which trickles through . For these fish water is not so plentiful and air rarely penetrates! The third bowl of fish are the worst off because they hardly get any food particles, water is scarce for so many, air is not there so many die from thirst and lack of air. Why is this story being told? It is the story of most of the poor countries on our planet.

This is also the story of Haiti.......this 3 bowl distribution has been going on for a long time and with the recent devastation, caused by the earthquake, who suffers most.....it is the people at the third level.

Facts And Figures

Just to quote a few facts for the reader to become enlightened on the situation in Haiti. Haiti was devastated on January 12, 2010 by the earthquake, causing destruction and displacing one million people. The epicentre of the earthquake was 15 miles WSW of Port-Au-Prince and was followed by 59 aftershocks. This was the worst earthquake since 1770 Port-Au-Prince has a population of 2,000,000 and the Haitian government estimated that 200,000 people have died and another 2,00,000 left homeless with 300,000 people in need of emergency help.

It is heartening to note that the whole world almost got into its act to send money and supplies to Haiti and this is commended. $195 million dollars in aid had been received with another $112 million dollars pledged $575 million has been collected by agencies like the World Food Program and UNICEF US Government has given $171 dollars in relief aid, USAID share of disaster assistance is $82 million and its office for Food for Peace contribution amounted $68 million Dominican Republic health assistance was $1 million 3 million meals have been delivered to 200,000 people but was not enough UN put aside $40 million for cash for work programs to help Haitians clear away the rubble 9,000 peace keepers in Haiti with another 3,500 to be sent soon. January 20th saw US military 2,000 troops on the ground helping with 2000 airborne personnel to reach. Additional 9,500 personnel are standing by US has flown 136 air missions bringing 2,400 tons of food and supplies and 1,900 passengers into Haiti January 19th saw 165,000 bottles of water and 152,000 litres of bulk water brought in for distribution US Navy's Nimitz class USS Carl Vinton is producing 100,000 gallons of drinkable water per day.

Water tanks are being built in different parts of the city.38.5 tons of water or 62,880 bottles of water have been distributed.14,500 meals ready to eat and 15,000 litres of water are scheduled to be air dropped China is to send $1 million , Ireland $5 million through relief agencies, France has pledged 65 clearing specialists, 6 sniffer dogs, 2 doctors and 2 nurses.

Netherlands will provide $2.9 million, Spain $4.3 million towards relief efforts, Italy sending medical personnel and a mobile field hospital. Recently Canada pledged $770 mil Haiti is considered the poorest Western Hemisphere country and has a population of 9 million people Port-au-Prince is the capital.

Facts and Figures courtesy Google Search Engine

Nagging Questions In Spite Of Help?

We can see that countries have tried their best to help, though it seems all this help is not enough. Unfortunately it is the story of the Fish........those at the bottom received no help and have perished or are struggling. One year after the earthquake, there are still 300,000 people in tents and without proper utilities.

One can ask the question Why is this? Are there any answers? Where did the bulk of the help go?

Where can we pinpoint the finger of accountability?

The Victims

The most urgent and dangerous fallout from the situation after the earthquake is that the help has not reached to certain sections of the people who are left unattended.

The most badly affected are children........left homeless, with parents dead, they are lost. Education has come to a halt. The danger here is that children are being used for smuggling and trafficking.

A recent report says that thousands of children are in orphanages but not all are orphans. Their parents leave them at the centres because they cannot afford to look after them. Where children are sent to work, they are treated like 'slaves'.

What Is The Priority And How Can We Help?

So the priority now is the children....they need all the basic necessities of life. There are groups working in Haiti to restore life to the poor people in the bottom of the fish bowl.

One way to help is to help sponsor the education of children which includes meals and clothes. Could a sponsorship program be initiated on the lines of other agencies, where families here could be in touch with children there in Haiti and help them be educated and stand on their feet??

As a reflection it is good to observe that this pattern of distribution of aid exists in many poor countries in the world. The time has come for countries to develop a Disaster Plan in all countries. UN ought to take the initiative in this. The Plan must envisage a proper receipt of the Aid, which needs documentation and a proper distribution. Governments of countries getting aid must adhere to certain norms. The questions posed above will never be answered, unless a plan is in hand for future and this means that people who contribute to the aid are frustrated or decide not to give help again. There ought to be accountability.

HAITI STILL HOPES.

I give below a Haitian's view:

"The earthquake startled me but provided a wake-up call". The concern is that much attention was given to Port-Au-Prince but people in Port A Paix were starving because they used to get their food and supplies through the capital city. Also the earthquake in Cayman islands and Guatemala are not isolated, though they may seem that way.

Talking to a young girl, Mickel,. She was sad and silent but very slowly began to speak to say that her family house came down like a ton of bricks, killing all in the house, parents and siblings. She was not in the house at that time but was terribly shaken. What was written on her face were years of endurance at the edge of society. She was hungry and emaciated with eyes large as saucers glaring out of a thin cheek-boned face! Her tears were dried, she could not cry any more.

She was taken to a shelter and there was helped to eat and revive. Meeting her after a week, she looked better and with a sad smile said she asked God for strength and courage to live on. She would study and work and rebuild.

THIS IS THE TRUE FACE OF HAITI……. Suffering, yes, but hopeful!! This type of hope is never out done by the earthquake on January 12, 2010.

KALEIDOSCOPE MEDLEY

C P R   EARPLUGS

It was a mystery how well sleep was coming to me these last few days, so that I did not need to use earplugs. Oh yes, of course, the reason is well known as CP R(Can./Pacific/Rail) is on 'strike'

A number of us live in Seniors' Buildings in Streetsville (a beautiful area to be in) and each night sleep gets interrupted. The rail car passes so close to Streetsville, where these Senior Apartments, Housing Complexes are. The complaint is not that CP passes there. In fact during the day it is quite picturesque as one sights the train meandering near given trees now that spring is here and summer not far behind.

What is most disturbing for most of us who cannot afford an air-conditioner which helps because all windows have to be closed, is the noise of the train. One stares at the ceiling in the middle of the night wondering why in these high tech days, when texting and computer, are done without noise, why these trains are so noisy.

I took a walk near the tracks and noticed that these trains are old and one seems to see them almost 100 years ago. They have not been improved like the GO! It is true, they carry goods, but these goods are vital for trade between US and Canada. The trains do need to run to carry goods to and fro but cannot someone discover a 'silencer' to keep the noise level down at night and the early hours of the morning? Can a homing device be installed whereby if objects are on the tracks, a signal would emerge to warn the train driver. I am not sure about this but the incidence of hearing aids seems to have increased its demands.

Sleep is sacred and noise is disturbing. Will some kind Techno do something about this.

FROM THE MOUTH OF BABES.......Your Torchlight!!

Have you ever been in the dark, groping for light. Maybe a torch light folding light,or pen light.

Try this since all these work with batteries. Put in the required batteries in the same way.....what happens....no light! Now try again, put in the batteries one way the other way.....complementary. Wow! there is light and you are happy.

The point I am introducing through this simple method is that 'marriage' for more than 2000 years has been between a man and woman in love but not only that, it is for the purpose of procreation to help the human race increase and multiply. Why? because true love always must be shared and within the marriage bond this sharing is fruitful in the children born.

Now let us take this further. The fact is that people of the same sex,whether men or women, will not and cannot bring about the fruit...the light...children. The 'batteries' are going the same way. Each partner in a marriage plays different roles to bring about an addition/s for the human race. People of the same sex joining together can be called by any other name except marriage, which is something special, delivered in a religious rite with a sense of commitment. Same sex 'error' alliances, which I call them, will intensify the 'darkness' on all fronts, which leaves people 'groping' for a way out.

Please give this serious thought and refrain from calling something 'unnatural' for whatever reason, by a sacred term known as 'marriage'.

I hope those who read this will see the light.

MEMORIES ARE MADE OF THESE

There is a saying that "Home is where the Heart is" and this is true for families who are spread over different continents for work or to better prospects for themselves and the future generations.

This saying can also be applied to millions of people from all over the world who emigrate to foreign lands for the sake of work and better prospects especially for their children. Though set up well in another country, the heart throbs and pulsates when memories of their homeland come to mind, especially for the older and not so older generations. This is true of the hundreds of people who have emigrated each year from India to Canada and who, at the drop of a hat, are willing to engage in anything that brings back these memories.

Each year in Canada, India's Independence Day, being 15th August, is hosted by Kamal and Rashmi Bhatia and their two sons Vashisht and Soham for friends and families. They go out of their way to open their home to hundreds of friends to celebrate this auspicious day.

Independence Day, 15 August 2011, brought to focus the 64 years since Independence from the British Raj. Streams of Indo-Canadians, men in their Indian dress, women in Saris, the younger generation in the modern version of 'salwar kameeze' as well as children, some dressed in Indian regalia, all assembled in the back lawn of the Bhatia house. This event is very participative and so we see people walking in with 'pot luck' Indian style. Though the sun was out in its splendor around 5 pm, people found chairs in the shade and in the sun without any discomfort.

The objective of the afternoon/evening was found in the invitation which went out to all the friends online reading as follows:

"India's Independence Day

Honor the Martyrs

Revel in its Culture and Diversity

Joy in the Resurgence of India"

JAI HIND

Honor to the Martyrs was focused and personalized in the main events in which Mahatma Gandhi participated in bringing about independence from the British. Soham, one of Kamal/Rashmi's son came on stage dressed like the Mahatma, while young adults both men and women took part in the reading of the events.

They recalled MK Gandhi's courage in opposing the 'raj' of the British which curbed the freedom of the Indian people.

August 15, 1947 was the date when this freedom was gained by the Indian nation but it was a struggle entailing pain and suffering and a series of violent events. As far back as 1857 a rebellion against the East India Company took place when the Indians demanded equal rights and the abolition of the landlord system in favor of the zamaderi land system.

1905 saw the partition of India by the British of one nation into two identities, which till today is the cause of unnecessary conflict. 1920 saw the non-cooperation movement. The civil disobedience movement in Jan 1930 accelerated the demand for freedom followed by the salt satyagarh and the dandi march with the Quit India call in 1942. These dates and events brought back the Memories which have made India. For the older generation present it was nostalgia and a reliving of a passion for freedom. For the younger generation, many who came at an early age, or were born in Canada, it was a refresher of what they had learned or read but also a tug at the heart strings, for home is where the heart belongs. The readings of these events were interspersed by patriotic songs rendered by fine and experienced artists.

Mahatma G (Soham who called himself the modern Gandhi) summed up the evening's enactments by remarking that freedom was sought and bought with much violence but besides this the real freedom is not just of the land (India) but of the mind. Freedom of the mind is the most essential element needed today in Indians and India and in the whole world. Kamal gave a vote of thanks to all those present for their participation. He confirmed that Canada is a land which each one of us present has adopted and he thanked Canada for its benefits which all present have enjoyed or are enjoying. He spoke of Peace and very vehemently expressed that Peace comes from the Heart and not the Head. He asked that we listen to what the heart calls us to do. He commended those present who are doing so much in this country but we need that extra step to move with the heart. He urged us as Indo Canadians to make a difference in our areas.

The first part of the program concluded with the flat hoisting and the singing of the National Anthem in Hindi. This was followed by a sumptuous spread of a variety of Indian cuisine and social interaction. I was very impressed with this family, Kamal, Rashmi, Vaishit and Soham. For the last 6 years they are organizing this celebration, with a fresh theme each year. There was present a group of young adults from College background and they were full of youthful energy, all appreciating their Indian background but youngsters who are free, creative and ongoing. There were Natasha, Clarissa, Roseanne and many others choosing careers in health, education and the sciences. What a lived example of Indo-Canadian culture in diversity. What I liked so much was their respect and acceptance of me…an elder.

In their company I felt 'young at heart'.

Supriya (thanks) to the Bhatia family for their initiative and leadership.

TELEPHONE MERRY GROUND

Have you ever been on a telephone ride round the world? Well it happened in this way.

My printer was making knocking noises though the printer was okay after it settled. (It still does!) Curious to know how to solve the problem, I phoned the number given on the Instruction Sheet, which incidentally was printed in China. I found myself talking to someone from US, who put me on to someone in the Philippines who put me on to someone in California who gave me the original telephone number, which got me to India. Wow! After a few pleasantries, since the location was in Calcutta (Kolkata), I was told that the calls were all free! (I hope so) The person from Calcutta informed me that they were giving out new printers at a discounted price and it would be sent to my doorstep. The old printer had to be put into a box/bag with a label and sent to a Courier who would return it, I suppose, to India?

I must say after this telephone merry-go--round with the problem not solved, I was totally exhausted and decided to post this on Word press.

Thank God it was a rainy day so I could spend all this time and energy indoors. Finally I decided to go to the outlet from which I originally purchased the printer and deal with them.

How very complicated can our lives get….simplification is urgent if we are to remain sane and creative. It strikes me: That's Globilization for you.

THE MYSTERY OF THE PINK NOTES

1/

There I was weak and tired
Just after surgery
A consoling visit, a handshake and a
Swift departure
I was left with a crisp pink note in my hand

2/

Sitting on a back bench
A lady comes by
A comforting smile , a thank you
And a crisp pink note…..I did not want it
She left it in my hand and moved on.

3/

A friend, a beautiful Christmas Card
Opened and appreciated
There again a crisp pink note
No, I can't take this…….
I'm not poor she said…I am rich in the Lord

4/

I sit and ponder: these notes are
all crisp and pink
Are they coming through a certain pipeline?
Who is the source?

5/

I ponder on our generous God
who is ever giving
But He has no hands…..only a big big heart
I know and believe He has an agent
Who arranges the gift of the crisp pink notes
The 50 dollar bills

6/

And so I again give the crisp pink notes in
The form of a monthly bulletin
To those who are the Treasures
of the Lord
Who by their pains and sufferings
Build His Kingdom to come

7/

Who is God's Agent…Who is God in disguise?
I think I know!!!

WAITING WAITING WAITING

For the rides that take me to church.
Doctors, groceries
Waiting, waiting ,waiting….sometimes on time, sometimes after time

Waiting. Waiting,waiting for the bus to arrive
In the heat, in the cold, in the harsh white lights from the cars
Which dazzle and distort one's eyes

Waiting, waiting, waiting for healing of surgery and scars
Both on the inside and the outside which only waiting can help
for healing takes time
What to do when one is waiting,
waiting,waiting
Write poems, do crosswords, reminiscene
read………keep cheerful don't complain
These numerous waiting times can make
one patient

Isn't this needed in waiting for Life's end
When waiting will be no more?

Edwards Brothers Malloy
Oxnard, CA USA
November 24, 2015